Baby
Goes to
Market

Baby

This one is for Nancy.
   A.

For David, Eva, and Fred with love
   A. B.

First U.S. edition 2017. ✿ Library of Congress Catalog Card Number 2017947990. ISBN 978-0-7636-9570-5. ✿ This book was typeset in Schinn. The illustrations were done in mixed media. ✿ Candlewick Press, 99 Dover Street, Somerville, Massachusetts 02144. visit us at www.candlewick.com.
Printed in Dongguan, Guangdong, China   18 19 20 21 22 TLF 10 9 8 7 6 5 4 3

Goes to Market

illustrated by
Atinuke ✪ Angela Brooksbank

CANDLEWICK PRESS

Baby goes to market
with Mama.

Market is very crowded.
Baby is very curious.

Baby is so curious that
Mrs. Ade, the banana seller,
gives Baby six bananas.

Baby is so surprised.

Baby eats one
banana . . .

and puts five bananas
in the basket.

Mama does not notice.
She is busy
buying rice.

Market is very crowded.
Baby is very hot.

Baby is so hot that
Mr. Femi, the orange seller,
gives Baby five juicy
oranges.

Baby grins.

Baby sucks one
orange . . .

and puts four oranges
in the basket.

Mama does not notice.
She is busy buying
homemade palm oil.

Market is very crowded.
Baby is very cheerful.

Baby is so cheerful that
Mr. Momo, the biscuit seller,
gives Baby four sugary
chin-chin biscuits.

Baby claps.

Baby eats one
chin-chin . . .

and puts three chin-chin
in the basket.

Mama does not notice.
She is busy buying
chili peppers.

Market is very crowded.
Baby is very funny.

Baby is so funny that
Mrs. Kunle, the
sweet-corn seller,
gives Baby
three roasted
sweet corn.

Baby
beams.

Baby eats one
roasted sweet corn . . .

and puts two roasted sweet corn in the basket.
Mama does not notice.
She is busy buying flip-flops.

Market is very crowded.
Baby is very naughty.
Very naughty, pulling
on ALL the clothes!

Baby is so sorry that
Mrs. Dele, the coconut seller, gives
Baby two pieces of coconut.

Baby licks his lips.

Baby eats
one piece of
coconut . . .

and puts the other piece
in the basket.

Mama does not notice.
Her basket is
very heavy.

Very, very
heavy.

And Mama thinks her
sweet baby must be
hungry by now!

"TAXI!"
Mama shouts.
"We need to get home
quick and fast!"

Mama puts her basket down.

"What is this?" cries Mama.
"Five bananas! Four oranges!
Three chin-chin biscuits!
Two roasted sweet corn!
One piece of coconut!
I did NOT buy
these!"

"No, you didn't!"

cries Mrs. Ade,
the banana seller,

and Mr. Femi,
the orange seller,

and Mr. Momo,
the chin-chin seller,

and Mrs. Kunle,
the sweet-corn seller,

and Mrs. Dele,
the coconut seller.

"We gave those things to Baby!"

Mama looks at Baby.

Baby laughs.

Mama laughs, too.

"What a good baby!" she says.
"You put all those things straight
into the basket!"

Mama rides the taxi.
Baby goes to sleep.
"Poor Baby!" says Mama.
"He's not had one
single thing
to eat!"